HE'S COMING! HE'S COMING!
BUT I'M NOT READY YET!
IS THIS ALL RIGHT? HOW DO I LOOK?
VERY PRETTY!
OH!!
GOOD DAY!
CARE FOR A SLICE OF CAKE, DEAREST HECTOR? PERHAPS TWO?
JUST ONE, THANKS. AND A CUP OF HOT CHOCOLATE, IF YOU'VE GOT SOME.
OH NO! I FORGOT TO WARM THE MILK!
ONE HOT CHOCOLATE COMING UP!
MMMMM, IT SMELLS DIVINE!
YOU'RE SUCH A GOOD FRIEND! THANKS!
YOU KNOW, YOU MADE QUITE AN IMPRESSION ON ME THE OTHER NIGHT AT THE BALL.
DID I?

...AND ME, DID YOU SEE ME? DID YOU LIKE MY OUTFIT?
VERY MUCH!
OH, MY SWEET... YOU'RE RAVISHING!!
OH, HECTOR...
PLOP!
A BIG GLOB OF SOMETHING JUST FELL INTO MY CUP...
REALLY?
SPLAT!
THERE!! ANOTHER ONE!
WH...WHAT'S GOING ON?
IT'S DRIPPING DOWN FROM EVERYWHERE!
HUH? BUT THIS ISN'T HOW THINGS WERE SUPPOSED TO TURN OUT!

THIS WAY!

YIKES!

SPLATCH!

BLECCCH!

HEY! GUYS, WHERE ARE YOU?

HELLO?!

!!

OH, NO!...DEAD END!
OOPS!
HAAAAAHHHH

SPLASH

Beautiful Darkness

Fabien Vehlmann & Kerascoët

Based on an original idea by Marie Pommepuy
Story by Marie Pommepuy & Fabien Vehlmann
Art by Kerascoët
Translated by Helge Dascher

DRAWN & QUARTERLY

YOOO-HOOO!

IS ANYBODY HERE?

YOO-HOO!
?!

HERE!

HEY!

?

UH...HELLO?

CRUNCH
CRUNCH

...THAT LOOKS REALLY GOOD.

I'M PRETTY HUNGRY TOO, AFTER EVERYTHING WE WENT THROUGH LAST NIGHT!

YOU KNOW, I WAS JUST ABOUT TO SERVE CAKE WHEN THE CEILING STARTED TO...?!

GO AHEAD, HELP YOURSELF.

HEY HO!
?!

WHOA! WHOA! WHOA! COOKIES! AWESOME!
THANKS, PLIM. I'M HAPPY TO SEE YOU, TOO.

HAVE YOU SEEN HECTOR? i HOPE HE'S OKAY.
NOPE, HAVEN'T SEEN HiM.
CAN i HAVE A COOKiE NOW?

WAiT, FiRST GO TELL THE OTHERS...LET THEM KNOW WE'VE FOUND FOOD.
OKAY, FiiiiiNE.

RUN, PLiM! FLY LiKE THE WiND!

HERE YOU GO!
THANKS!

AND THIS IS FOR YOU...
OH, THANK YOU!

FASTER, PLIM! LET'S NOT MAKE THESE POOR PEOPLE WAIT!
I'M... ARGH... TRYING!
CRRR

OH, LOOK AT THAT LITTLE CUTIE! HERE'S TWO NICE PIECES FOR YOU!!
GAH!
HOW KIND OF YOU!

WE DON'T WANT HIM GOING HUNGRY.

HECTOR?

PLIM, CAN I LEAVE YOU TO HANDLE THE REST?
WITH PLEASURE!

BE SURE TO MAKE THE PORTIONS EVEN SO IT'S NICE AND FAIR.
UNDERSTOOD!

I'M SO SO HUNGRY.
!!

HECTOR?

C'MON, LET'S GO EAT.
NAAW!

JEEZ, COME ON!
NAAAH!!
YOU'RE SUCH A PAIN!

HECTOR!

MY DEAR, HERE YOU ARE.
I WONDERED WHAT HAPPENED TO YOU.

WERE YOU WORRIED ABOUT ME?
NO, I...WELL, MAYBE A BIT.

OH, YOU SHOULDN'T HAVE. I CAN TAKE CARE OF MYSELF YOU KNOW.
BUT THIS WHOLE SITUATION IS SO STRANGE!

i'VE TAKEN CHARGE THOUGH, YOU KNOW?
OH YEAH?

YES. i'VE BEEN HANDING OUT FOOD... AND i... UH...
NO KIDDING?

AH, i THINK THERE'S A PROBLEM OVER THERE! i'LL GO SEE WHAT'S UP!

GOOD THING i'M HERE OR NOTHING WOULD GET DONE.
SEE YOU LATER!

OUCH, OUCH! MY ANKLE!!
SHH, iT'S ALL RIGHT. WHAT'S GOiNG ON?

i... i FELL, TRYING TO GET AWAY FROM THAT AWFUL THiNG!
OVER THERE! iT'S HORRiBLE!!
PROTECT ME!
?!

...

iT DOESN'T SEEM VERY MEAN TO ME.

i'LL SHOVE iT OVER THERE, JUST iN CASE.
BOP

OH! THANK YOU!! YOU SAVED MY LiFE!
iT'S NOTHiNG, REALLY!

YOU SHOULDN'T STAY OUT HERE iN THE SUN, THOUGH. YOU'LL GET HEAT STROKE.
BUT i CAN'T WALK! iT HURTS TOO MUCH!

BOO-HOO!
HMM

i GUESS WE COULD MAKE A LiTTLE TENT WiTH THiS. COME HELP ME.

HERE, LET'S GET iT OVER HER, LiKE THAT.
MFF
Aurora
HEY!

Aurora
WHO'S AURORA?

i AM.

OH, ALL RiGHT.

OKAY, YOU CAN MAKE MORE LiTTLE SHELTERS. i'LL GO HAVE A LOOK AROUND.

UH...THAT'S ENOUGH FOR TODAY.

STOMP
AAAAH!!
SCRITCH
SCRATCH
BANG!
SNIF
SNIF

STOMP
STOMP

EEE!!!...

AAAAAAH!

AAAARGHHHH

AAAAAH

NO!! DON'T

GNNT

WHAT A MESS!
WE'VE GOT NOTHING LEFT TO EAT!

OH! PLIM,
I'M SO HAPPY!

PLIM!!
DO I KNOW YOU?

...WE COULD USE
SOME ROPE.
HEY, I
KNOW!

NAAAH!!

HEE HEE

WHHAA!

?
WHWHWH
WHAAA!!

HEY THERE, WHAT'S WRONG?
ARE YOU SAD?
EHEUHEU!

WHERE'S YOUR MOMMA?
DID SHE DISAPPEAR?
EHEU!

DON'T WORRY, BABY,
I'LL TAKE CARE OF YOU.

GOO!

FRRRTCH...

BZZZZZZ

HEE HEE!
THAT TICKLES!

THIS IS FUN!...
I'M HUNGRY.

WE'RE HUNGRY TOO, YOU KNOW...MAYBE AURORA WILL FIND FOOD FOR US TODAY.

MAYBE SHE'LL BRING BACK BERRIES, LIKE LAST TIME.
YEAH! AND MUSHROOMS!!

NO, WE SAID NO MORE MUSHROOMS, REMEMBER? SOME OF THEM ARE DEADLY.
OH, RIGHT, THAT'S TRUE. POOR JOSEPHINE, MARGO, AND AGATHA. I LIKED THEM.

AND POOR SWEETIE, ADELAIDE, AND MIMI...
AND JUJU AND ASTRID, TUBBY, CELESTE, AND STINKER.
...AND WILSON.

SO HUNGRY.
YOU KNOW WHAT? WE NEED TO FIND OTHER THINGS TO EAT...
SURE, BUT WHAT?

I MEAN, WE CAN'T BE LIKE THAT PIG. GROSS!

EATING FLIES AND MAGGOTS!
DISGUSTING!
SO SO HUNGRY.

HEY! WH...??

WHAT DID YOU JUST DO!?

WANNA PLAY? LOOK, IT'S LIKE I'M PREGNANT.
HA HA! ALL RIGHT!

OH!! I CAN FEEL THE BABY MOVE!
CALL ME MOMMY!

iK iK iiiK!
OH, UH...NO THANKS, i'LL PASS ON THE MUD. i'M NOT HUNGRY ANYMORE.

BUT i'D BE GLAD TO TAKE A FEW BERRiES HOME!

THANKS SO MUCH FOR HAViNG ME!
i NEED TO GO NOW.
!

TAPATA TAPATAP

SKEEEK! EEEEK!

DON'T WORRY, i'LL BE BACK LATER. i PROMiSE.

THERE, THAT'S BETTER, HUH?

SHE'S BACK!

ARE YOU OKAY? DiD THE MOUSE TRY TO SCRATCH YOU WiTH HiS POiNTY CLAWS?
NO, NO, EVERYTHiNG WAS FiNE.

DON'T EAT THEM ALL! LEAVE SOME FOR THE OTHERS.
HURRAY!

HE'S STRANGE, BUT HE'S KiND. i BET HE'S GLAD TO HAVE NEW NEiGHBORS!

iN ANY CASE, i THiNK HE'LL HELP US FiND MORE STRAWBERRiES...
YOU'RE THE BEST! YOU EVEN UNDERSTAND MOUSE LANGUAGE!

STOP COPYING ME ALL THE TIME!

THIS IS MY IDEA! GO AWAY!!

MPFF...

THAT WAS A REALLY GREAT IDEA!
YEAH...REALLY!

GRMMMBBLE

CHEEP
CHEEP

CHEEP
CHEEP
CHEEP
CHEEP

CHEEP
CHEEP

CHEEP

CHEEP
CHEEP
RRHHH

i GUESS iT WASN'T SUCH A GOOD iDEA AFTER ALL.
NO, iT REALLY WASN'T SUCH A GOOD iDEA.

?

MiND NOT REPEATiNG EVERYThiNG i SAY?

ALL CLEAR! NO DANGER iN SIGHT!!

HOW ABOUT A SHAKE?

C'MON, GiMME!

SNAP

NOW THE OTHER ONE, C'MON!

OH! HELLO!

WE KEEP MEETING, BUT WE'VE NEVER INTRODUCED OURSELVES. I'M AURORA!

I... I'M T-TIMOTHY...
YOU KEEP TO YOURSELF A LOT. YOU SHOULD COME JOIN US AT THE CAMP.

NO... THE OTHERS SCARE ME...

THERE'S NO NEED TO BE AFRAID!
NO... ACTUALLY, YES... I'M DIFFERENT FROM THE OTHERS. I FEEL LIKE SOMETHING BAD COULD HAPPEN...

DON'T WORRY, TIMOTHY. I PROMISE, NOTHING BAD WILL EVER HAPPEN AGAIN. YOU HAVE MY WORD.

I'M DOING EVERYTHING I CAN TO MAKE THINGS LIKE THEY WERE BEFORE. TRUST ME?
UH... YES.

I'M GOING TO GO NOW. BUT IF YOU GET TOO LONELY, COME JOIN US, ALL RIGHT?

OKAY.

C'MON!
LET'S GO!
WHAT DO YOU ALL THINK YOU'RE DOING?

WE'RE TRYING TO TEACH HIM TRICKS!
BUT... HOW COME?

...

HEY! HOW ABOUT WE HUNT FOR PEBBLES?!

YEAAHH! LET'S GO LOOK FOR PEBBLES!!

HELLO.
HELLO.

WHAT'S WRONG WITH YOUR HAND?
I SCRATCHED MYSELF ON A PLANT. IT'S SUPER ITCHY.

OKAY, I'LL KEEP AN EYE ON THE PLANTS, TOO.
WOULD YOU? THANKS.

i CAN'T SEE NATALiE...THE HOLE FiLLED UP WiTH WATER LAST NiGHT.
TOO BAD, iT ACTUALLY LOOKED LiKE A GOOD SHELTER.

THERE SHE iS...

OOPS. DARN.
CAN WE GO NOW?
BLOB

YOU FiSHiNG? ANY NiBBLES? CAN i JOiN?
iF YOU LiKE. JUST TAKE THAT FiSHiNG ROD...
BUT GO FARTHER DOWN. THiS iS OUR SPOT.

OKAY. THANKS!

YOU FiSHiNG? ANY NiBBLES? CAN i JOiN?
...

?
SHE'S WEiRD. C'MON, LET'S GO.

iT'S ALL YOUR FAULT! STOP COPYiNG ME!
YOU'RE THE ONE THAT'S COPYiNG!

THE ANTS GO MARCHING ONE BY ONE,
HURRAH! HURRAH!
THE ANTS GO MARCHING ONE BY ONE
HURRAH! HURRAH!

HI, AURORA! HOW'S THE BERRY PICKING GOING?
UH, ALL RIGHT... AND THE HUNTING?

GREAT! OF COURSE, YOU'VE GOT TO BE PATIENT...STAGS AND WILD BOARS ARE QUICK AND SMART. YOU CAN'T JUST WALK UP TO THEM.

BUT TRUST ME... CHOMP CHOMP...WE'LL ALL BE EATING A NICE ROAST IN NO TIME!
I DON'T DOUBT IT FOR A SECOND.

AURORA, I'VE BEEN WANTING TO SAY...
YES?

WE HAVEN'T SEEN EACH OTHER AS MUCH AS I'D LIKE THESE LAST FEW DAYS...

BUT YOU'RE ALWAYS ON MY MIND, EVERY MOMENT OF THE DAY! EVEN IN THE HEAT OF THE CHASE, MY THOUGHTS RUSH TO YOU!
!!

PRINCE!! I...
NO, NOT NOW!

I HEAR THE PANTING OF A WILD BEAST, READY TO TAKE FLIGHT, HOOFS PAWING THE GROUND!

COME, MY FAITHFUL COMPANIONS! LET US GIVE CHASE!!

LET US NOT TARRY! BEHOLD, A SHORTCUT!

ONWARD!!
THWACK
THWOCK
THWACK

GOOD LUCK!

THWACK!
THWOCK!
THWACK
THWACK

I'VE GOT A BLISTER. I SUGGEST WE TAKE A BREAK.
YES, PRINCE!

HOW'S iT GOiNG?

FiNE. DON'T WORRY, i'VE GOT EVERYTHiNG UNDER CONTROL.
HERE, HAVE SOME BERRiES.

NO THANKS...KEEP THEM FOR THOSE WHO NEED THEM MOST.
OH, THAT'S SO NiCE OF YOU!

PLiM, i WANTED TO TELL YOU...YOU KNOW, i REALLY APPRECiATE EVERYTHiNG YOU'RE DOiNG.

WE COULDN'T MANAGE WiTHOUT YOU...THANKS, HUH? FROM THE BOTTOM OF MY HEART...
DON'T MENTiON iT.

WHEN WE'RE DONE, i'LL GET SOME WOOD TO FORTiFY OUR SHELTER. WE'LL BE NiCE AND SAFE.
GOOD iDEA!

SLURP!
PLOP
PLOP

WELL, HELLO, AURORA! HOW DO YOU LIKE MY DRESS?

iT'S VERY PRETTY.

i KNOW! i'M MAKiNG iT WiTH FLY WiNGS... iT'S TAKiNG FOR-EV-ER.

iT LOOKS LiKE A WEDDiNG GOWN!
DOES iT? i HADN'T NOTiCED!

BUT THEN...iT'S DARK iN HERE. iT'S HARD TO SEW PROPERLY.

iF YOU LiKE, i'LL TRY TO PUT iN SOME WiNDOWS TOMORROW.
CAN'T YOU DO iT SOONER? OH WELL, i GUESS YOU'RE DOiNG YOUR BEST.

SEE YOU TOMORROW!

SWEET BUT A BiT SLOW ON THE UPTAKE.
HEE HEE HEE!
PPFFF!

i'M HUNGRY...

HELLO.
HELLO, PLiM.

WiTH THE STATE YOU'RE iN, i BETTER WATCH YOUR PORTiON SO NOBODY STEALS iT FROM YOU.
HUH?

THAT'S SO NiCE OF YOU!
CHOMP

WOW! COOL!

YEAH, SUPER DUPER COOL!
EXCEPT WE NEED MORE BUTTONS.

LET'S GO FiND BUTTONS!!
YEAAH!

LA LA LA LI LA LA
LA LA LI LI
LA LA
TRA LA LA
OH!
HEE HEE HEE!
OUCH!!
HEY!

IT WAS HIGH TIME FOR A BATH.
AND MY DRESS IS ALL STAINED.

OH!
FLAP FLAP

HAVE YOU COME TO
FRESHEN UP AS WELL?

WAIT!...
FLAPFLAPFLAP

?
TAPATAPATAP

AAH!!

BRAAM!

SKRAAATCH!
SKRAAATCH!

SKRATCH
SKRATCH
SKRATCH

THE THING I LIKED ABOUT YOU RIGHT AWAY IS, YOU'RE COOL. YOU'RE SUPER COOL!
THAT'S RIGHT.

BECAUSE I... HUH?! PLIM!

YEAH? WHAT'S THE MATTER?
O...ON YOUR...SHOULDER!!

HOLD STILL! IT COULD STING YOU!
!!

I'LL MAKE IT COME THIS WAY! HEY! HEEEY!

YOO-HOO!!

IT'S WORKING!! I'M GONNA GET IT AS FAR AWAY AS POSSIBLE!

DON'T WORRY ABOUT ME, PLIM! I...I CAN MANAGE!
EEEEE!!

HEY, YOU! COME CARRY MY WOOD!

LEMME HAVE iT! COME ON, GiMME!
C'MON, GiVE iT TO ME!
FiNE, YOU'RE SUCH A PAiN.

HOLD ON TiGHT!
GiMME! GiMME!

?
!

HEY! GiVE iT BACK!!
iT'S MiNE NOW! NO TAKE BACKS. YOU LOSE!

KNOW WHAT?...

THE OTHER DAY, A BiRD SETTLED RiGHT NEXT TO ME!

THiS CLOSE!
NO WAY!

A BIT OF MOSS ON THE GROUND AND IT'LL BE PERFECT.

HECTOR WILL BE HAPPY.
I THINK HE'S GOING TO LIKE IT HERE.

BUT ENOUGH TALK. THERE'S LOTS MORE HOUSES TO BUILD!

EVERYBODY NEEDS A LITTLE HOUSE, IT'S IMPORTANT...

I DON'T LIKE THAT FLY.
HOW COME?

HEY, AURORA...
WHY ARE YOU CRYING?

?!...I DON'T KNOW...

AURORA?
...I DON'T FEEL SO GOOD.

EEEEEEEE!!!

EEEEE

HHHH...HHHH
NIGHTMARE...

HHH...HHHH
NIGHTMARE!

WHEW!

RiSE AND
SHiiiNE!!

HALT!
HEY, NiCE
HEADDRESS.
HAND iT OVER.

...MMMH i'M
THiRSTY...
i...i'LL GO
GET SOME DEW
WATER.

STiLL STUCK?
iT'S BEEN SiX DAYS.
i TOLD HER iT
WAS TOO SMALL.
HALT!
i KNOW, BUT SHE
REALLY WANTED
TO HAVE TEA WiTH
NADiNE AND PiPPA.

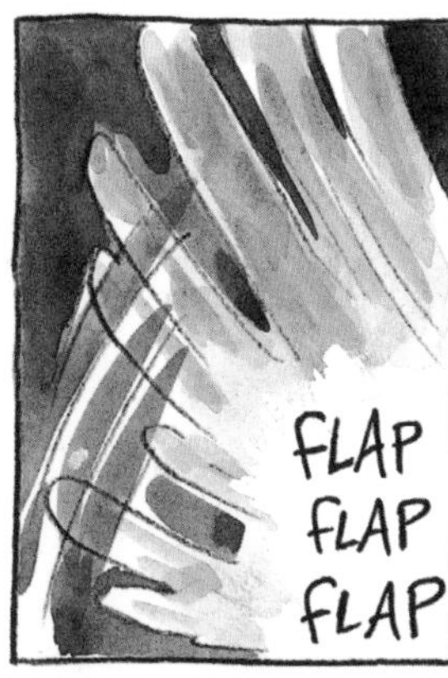
FLAP
FLAP
FLAP

FLAP FLAP

WAIT, I'M COMING!

HOW CAN I HELP?
THE SCISSORS!

NOW, CUT!

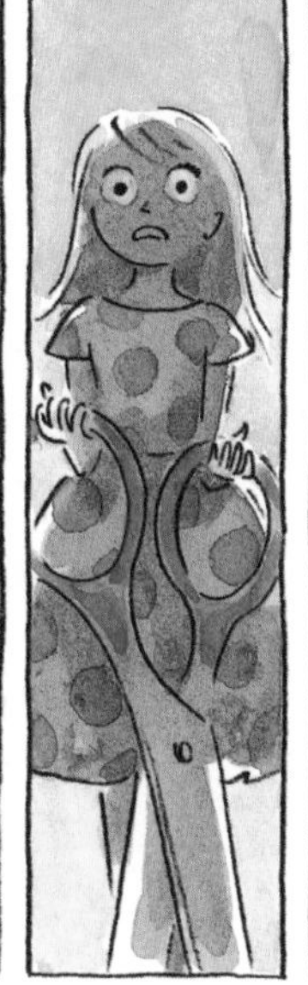

CUT THE WING, FAST!

CR...
CRATCH!

NOW THIS ONE, HURRY!

SCREEETCH!

HE WON'T BE ABLE TO GO VERY FAR.

I'LL FINISH TAMING HIM WHEN HE GETS TIRED OF HOPPING AROUND.

YOU'RE LEAVING FOR GOOD THIS TIME, AREN'T YOU?

THE OTHERS ARE LUCKY TO HAVE YOU, YOU KNOW.

HAVE YOU FOUND IT?
HOLD ON!
MPF

HA!

BUT IT'S NOT GLOWING!

WAIT!

AAAAAH!

WHAT'S THAT?

I'M THROWING A PARTY.
A PARTY?
FOR US AND THE FOREST ANIMALS.
Plim
Zelie

HERE, THIS IS YOUR INVITATION.
Plim

YOU NEED TO COME, OKAY? WE'VE GOT TO MEET OUR NEIGHBORS IF WE ALL WANT TO GET ALONG.

HNNFFF!

SBLURF!

i GUESS iT WAS ROTTEN.
LOOK, THAT ONE'S BETTER!
HEY! YOU TWO!

C'MERE, SiNCE YOU'RE NOT DOiNG ANYTHiNG. ZELiE NEEDS HELP SEWiNG HER DRESS.

UH, ACTUALLY, WE'RE BUSY... WE'RE CHOOSiNG A GiFT FOR AURORA.
iT'S TO THANK HER FOR iNViTiNG US TO HER FOREST PARTY!

COME ON! THiS'LL TAKE TWO MiNUTES! DON'T BE SO SELFiSH!

FiNE, SETTLED. FOLLOW ME.
WHAT?...OKAY, BUT...

UHH...CAN YOU BRiNG THE APPLE TO AURORA, PLEASE?

A SEED WOULD DO TOO. i THiNK i'D LiKE iT iF SOMEONE GAVE ME A SEED.

HEY, YOU! WHAT'RE YOU DOING HERE?

I SEE...AURORA GAVE YOU AN INVITATION TOO.
Timothy

BUT YOU'RE NOT GOING TO THE PARTY LIKE THAT, ARE YOU? YOU LOOK LIKE A BEGGAR. HERE, I'LL DO YOUR HAIR.

UH, NO, I...

C'MON...YOU DON'T WANT TO HURT AURORA'S FEELINGS, DO YOU?

DON'T MOVE! iT'S HARD ENOUGH ALREADY TO GET THE KNOTS OUT... WHAT DO YOU DO, MOP THE FLOOR WiTH YOUR HAiR?
HA HA HA

WHAT A CUTE BABY! CAN i HAVE iT, ZELiE?
SURE, SWEETiE PiE. HE'S ALL YOURS!

THERE! LOOK AT WHAT YOU MADE ME DO!
OUCH!

LET'S TRY THE OTHER SiDE NOW.
NO!
STOP! DON'T BE SUCH A FUSSPOT!
NO!

OH!

AND WE THOUGHT YOU WERE NORMAL!!

I...I'M A MONSTER.

I DON'T DESERVE TO LIVE HERE, WITH ALL OF YOU.
WELL, THAT'S TRUE!

HEY, I'VE GOT AN IDEA! YOU TWO, GET THE PENCIL CASE. WE'LL HAVE A BURIAL! THIS WILL BE GREAT.

...OKAY, LIE DOWN INSIDE, AND YOU'LL BE DEAD.
...ALL RIGHT...

NOW COVER HER WITH EARTH.

I'LL PRETEND TO PRAY.

MNMMMNMMMMNNNNMMNNNMMNN

THAT'S ONE CEREMONY DONE. VERY, VERY GOOD.
WHAT DO WE DO NOW?

IT'S LATE...LET'S GO HOME.
GOO?

C'MON, JUST A BIT FARTHER!!
OUFF!

MPFF!
FRRRRRR

THERE...

I'M HERE! I'VE BROUGHT A LATECOMER.

...THE OTHERS HAVEN'T ARRIVED?

PLIM, HECTOR, TIMOTHY...THEY PROMISED THEY'D BE HERE!

AURORA, DON'T YOU THINK WE SHOULD JUST EAT AND GO?...
NO, NO, WE'LL WAIT A BIT LONGER...
I'M SURE THEY'LL BE HERE ANY MOMENT.

EXCEPT IT'LL BE DARK. THAT'S TOO BAD.

WAIT!!

NOT YET!
BACK OFF!

I SAID, WAIT!

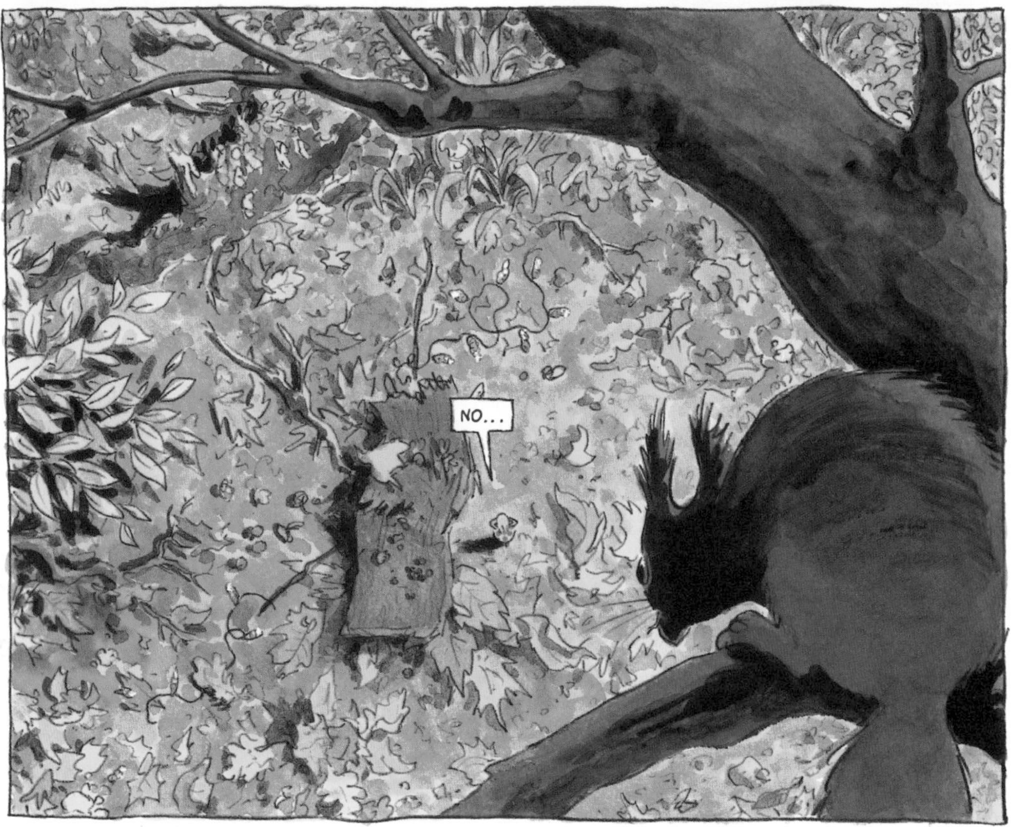
NO...

MMM♩♪MMM♫♩

Hi, ZELiE.
HEY, AURORA...

SO, HOW'S THE PARTY COMiNG ALONG?
...?

ARE YOU SURE?...
iT...iT WAS YESTERDAY!
YOUR iNViTATiON WASN'T CLEAR ABOUT THE DATE.

HERE, HAVE A SEAT AND TELL ME HOW iT WENT.
iT WAS TERRiBLE! THE ANiMALS BEHAVED LiKE... LiKE BEASTS!

ONE OF THEM EVEN PEED ON THE TABLE!

AND NOBODY CAME, NOT EVEN TiMOTHY! EVEN THOUGH i SPE-CifiCALLY TOLD HER THE TiME.
HOW THOUGHTLESS! YOU MUST HAVE FELT HUMiLiATED.

HECTOR DiDN'T COME EiTHER!
OH!

GET ME SOME THREAD, WOULD YOU?

AURORA, YOU KNOW HOW BOYS CAN BE...I'M SURE HECTOR DIDN'T MEAN TO UPSET YOU.
YOU THINK?

I'M CERTAIN. HE PROBABLY MISUNDER-STOOD, THAT'S ALL.

YOU KNOW WHAT? I'LL GO TALK TO HIM! MAYBE THAT'LL REASSURE YOU.
OH!

THANKS, ZELIE, TH-THAT'S VERY KIND OF YOU.
DON'T THANK ME YET! YOU NEVER KNOW WITH MEN...

?
IT'S STARTING, HURRY!!

WHAT DO YOU MEAN? WHAT'S STARTING?
HUUURRY!
HEE HEE HEE!!

COME ON, WHAT IS IT?
THERE, SEE FOR YOUR-SELF!

LONG LIVE
THE NEWLYWEDS!
LONG LIVE
THE NEWLYWEDS!

LONG LIVE THE NEWLYWEDS!
HURRAY!
HURRAY!

OH, LOOK WHO'S HERE!

GOOD, CUZ WE'VE GOT SOMETHING FOR YOU.
GO AWAY. I DON'T WANT TO SEE ANYBODY.

HEY, GUYS, OVER HERE!!

WE CAUGHT THE MOUSE!
ZELIE SAID YOU WANTED TO GET EVEN!
GO AHEAD, WE'LL HOLD HIM!

WHAT'RE YOU WAITING FOR?!
DO YOU WANT HIM TO PEE ON YOU AGAIN OR WHAT?
HEE HEE HEE!
HA HA!
DO IT!!

...LOOK AT YOU, YOU BAD MOUSE!!

HEY, HEAR THAT?
YOU MUST BE REAL BAD!

I'M TERRIBLY DISAPPOINTED IN YOU! YOU...

YOU... YOU RUINED MY PARTY!!
YEAH!
YOU DIRTY STINKER!

WICKED!!
EEK!

WICKED MOUSE!!
SKREEEE!

SUPER!
HA HA, WHO'S PROUD NOW, HUH?!

GOODBYE, PRINCESS PEE-PEE! HA HA!
C'MON, LET'S CHASE THE MOUSE!
YEEAAHHH!

GO TELL THE OTHERS WE FOUND FOOD.

OKAY...BURP...LET'S FIND ZELIE.
I KEPT THE HEART FOR HER.

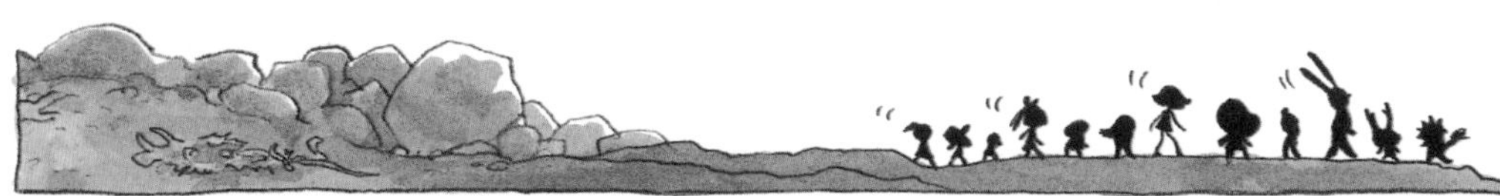

POK
POK
POK

POK
POK
POK

POK
POK
POK
POK
POK
POK
POK

OH, NO...
HECTOR! MY RIBBON!
?

MY RIBBON FELL IN THE WATER! YOU NEED TO GO GET IT FOR ME!
REALLY?

HECTOR, I'VE GOT TO HAVE IT! I FEEL NAKED WITHOUT IT!!

BUT iT'S VERY FAR, AND i DON'T SEE HOW i CAN—
YOU'RE MY PRINCE, SO YOU HAVE TO SERVE ME, DON'T YOU?
UH...

YES, OF COURSE! i... i'M YOUR PRINCE!

i KNEW iT! LET'S HAVE A FINE BOAT FOR HECTOR!

UGH, ARE YOU EVEN TRYiNG?!

WHAT'S TAKiNG SO LONG?!
iT'S THAT... i BETTER NOT FALL iN, i CAN'T...

?!!

THERE'S SOMETHiNG iN THE WATER!!
HECTOR, ENOUGH. JUST GET THE RiBBON!
SPLASH
SPLASH
SPLASH
SPLASH

AAAHH!!
PLUNK

THAT iDIOT!...
BRiNG HiM BACK.

OH, DEAR.

BURP!

DOES HE AT LEAST HAVE MY RiBBON?
SLURB
PLOTCH!

HERE, I'VE GOT IT!

I EMPTIED IT. EXCEPT FOR SOME SMALL SCRATCHES INSIDE, IT'S LIKE NEW.
VERY GOOD. IT WOULD HAVE BEEN UNFAIR TO GIVE HECTOR LESS OF A CEREMONY THAN TIMOTHY.

NOW, LET US GRIEVE THE SAD FATE OF MY DECEASED HUSBAND.

HECTOR!

BOO HOO HOO HOO HECTOR!
POOR ZELIE!

WHAT'RE YOU DOING HERE?

I DON'T WANT TO LIVE WITH THE OTHERS ANYMORE.

COME.

YOU CAN SPEND THE NIGHT HERE, BUT NOT A SOUND.
HE'S RIGHT NEXT DOOR.

LOOK FOR YOURSELF.

!

HELLO, JANE!

DO YOU LIKE IT?

...YOU GOT THIS IN HIS HOUSE, DIDN'T YOU?

YOU DON'T HAVE TO WORRY. I WAS CAREFUL.
I'M TELLING YOU, HE'S DANGEROUS.

...AND HE STINKS WORSE THAN ANYTHING!!
HE DOES?

THE SOONER I FIND ANOTHER PLACE, THE BETTER.
...IT'LL BE DIFFICULT, AS LONG AS IT'S SO COLD OUT.

AT LEAST IT'S WARM HERE, AND THERE'S FOOD.

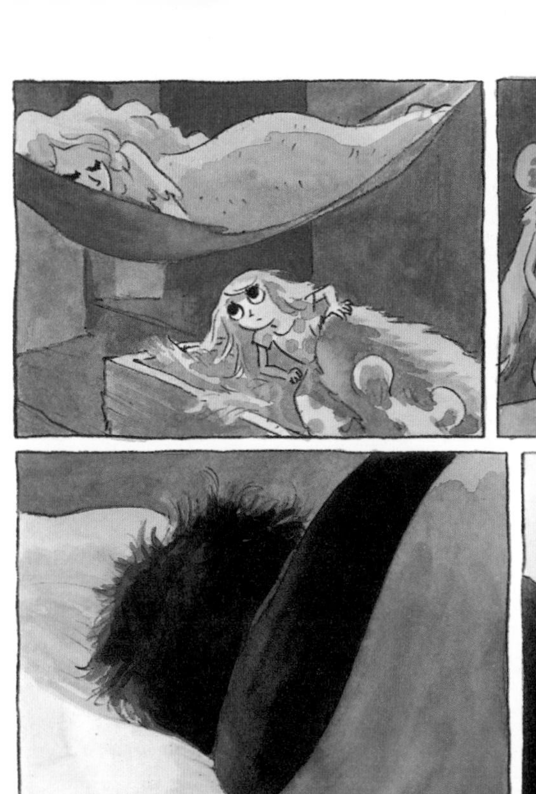

i LIKE THIS SMELL.
iT'S STRONG, BUT SWEET, TOO.
iT SMELLS LiKE HONEY!

PLIC

SCRATCH
SCRATCH

JANE! i SAW SOMETHiNG! COME QUiCK!!

WHAT ARE YOU TALKiNG ABOUT?
JUST COME, PLEASE!!

iS iT ZELiE?
...THEY'RE HEADED THiS WAY.

AND THOSE iDiOTS ARE SiNGiNG... THEY'LL GiVE US AWAY!

JANE?!
STAY HERE... i'LL TRY TO DO SOMETHiNG!

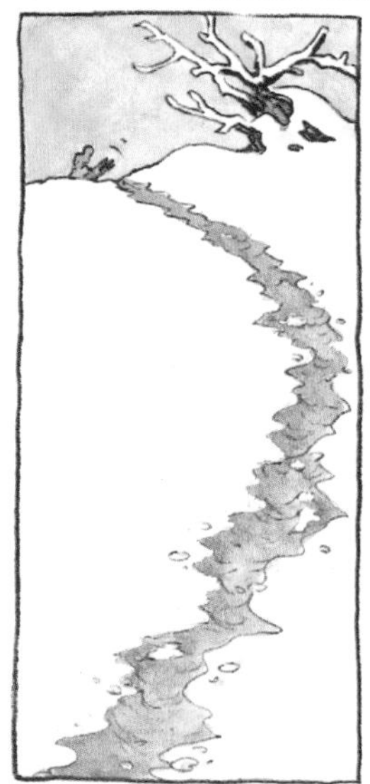

JANE, WAiT FOR ME!

?!

AURORA, WHAT A SURPRISE!

WE THOUGHT YOU WERE DEAD.
...WHERE IS JANE? THAT'S HER ROBIN.
JANE? DON'T KNOW HER.

HELLO, AURORA!...

WHAT A DUMP. WE'LL NEED TO FIX IT UP, QUICK.

AT LEAST IT'S WARMER IN HERE THAN OUTSIDE.

YOU CAN'T STAY HERE! ...THIS IS MY PLACE...

NO! NOT THERE!

IT'S DANGEROUS. THAT'S WHERE HE LIVES! THE...THE GIANT. HE'S VERY MEAN!...
IT'S MUCH WARMER HERE!

ZELIE!
YOU NEED TO CALL HER PRINCESS NOW.

IT'S BEST TO KEEP QUIET OR THEY'LL MAKE YOU MISERABLE. BUT I'LL BE YOUR FRIEND.

YOO-HOO!

HEY! PSSST!!

THE GIANT'S COMING!

THIS WILL MAKE A VERY NICE HOUSE...

...WITH A GIANT, JUST FOR ME!

YOU'RE BACK, FINALLY.

WE FIGURED HUNGER WOULD GET THE BEST OF YOU.

YOU'RE TOO LATE, THERE'S NOTHING LEFT. THAT'LL TEACH YOU.

YOU KNOW, AURORA, YOU NEED TO DO WHAT YOU'RE TOLD IF YOU WANT TO STAY HERE WITH US.

YOU CAN START BY WASHING OUR BOOTS...AND THEY BETTER BE DRY BY TOMORROW.

DID YOU HEAR HER?
SHUSH, PLIM. I'LL HELP HER. SHE'S NOT USED TO THIS YET.

YOU'LL SEE, IT'S EASY ENOUGH ONCE YOU ADJUST!
THANKS...

WAIT, I'LL BE BACK...

PLIM, I NEED TO TALK TO YOU!
I'M BORED ALREADY.

I KNOW A SECRET PLACE... I'D LIKE TO SHARE IT WITH YOU, LIKE BEFORE, BUT IN EXCHANGE YOU NEED TO HELP ME KEEP IT SECRET FROM ZELIE, OKAY?

MAYBE.

I'LL BE YOUR SERVANT TOO, IF YOU LIKE.
OKAY THEN. WHERE IS IT?

IT'LL BE OUR VERY OWN SECRET, ALL RIGHT? PROMISE?
CROSS MY HEART AND HOPE TO DIE.

THERE'S NOBODY. NOW'S THE MOMENT!

OVER HERE, ZELIE!

HEY, THIS IS NICE!

AND IT'S SO MUCH WARMER THAN THAT DINGY SHED.

AURORA WAS HIDING IT!

THAT WASN'T VERY SMART.

BUT YOU'VE NEVER BEEN TOO BRIGHT, HAVE YOU?...THAT'S YOUR PROBLEM, AURORA.

I'LL THINK OF A PUNISHMENT...TO SET AN EXAMPLE.

SPECS, COME GIVE ME A MASSAGE!

YES, PRINCESS. COMING.

AURORA?
KLONG!

CLACK!

HEY, WHAT'S
ALL THIS?

I'LL NEED TO REBUILD MY LITTLE NEST...

IT'S ALL RIGHT. I'VE GOT PLENTY OF TIME.

THAT MEAL YOU'RE MAKING FOR US SMELLS GOOD.

MY SWEET PRINCE.

 Originally published in French as *Jolies Ténèbres* by Dupuis. Translator: Helge Dascher. Translation editor: John Kadlecek. Title design: Ray Fenwick.

drawnandquarterly.com

First hardcover edition: February 2014. Second hardcover printing: April 2014. Third hardcover printing: February 2015. Fourth hardcover printing: June 2015. First paperback edition: October 2018. Second paperback printing: May 2021. Third paperback printing: October 2022. 10 9 8 7 6 5 4 3. Printed in China.

Cataloguing data available from Library and Archives Canada.

Cet ouvrage a bénéficié du soutien des Programmes d'aide à la publication de l'Institut français.

Drawn & Quarterly acknowledges the support of the Government of Canada and the Canada Council for the Arts for our publishing program, and the National Translation Program for Book Publishing, an initiative of the Roadmap for Canada's Official Languages 2013–2019: Education, Immigration, Communities, for our translation activities.

Drawn & Quarterly reconnaît l'aide financière du gouvernement du Québec par l'entremise de la Société de développement des entreprises culturelles (SODEC) pour nos activités d'édition. Gouvernement du Québec—Programme de crédit d'impôt pour l'édition de livres—Gestion SODEC

Published in the USA by Drawn & Quarterly, a client publisher of Farrar, Straus and Giroux. Published in Canada by Drawn & Quarterly, a client publisher of Raincoast Books. Published in the United Kingdom by Drawn & Quarterly, a client publisher of Publishers Group UK.